Remembering Barbara Niblett, who made
Burford Playgroup a happy place — J.W.

First American edition published in 2001 by Carolrhoda Books, Inc.

Text copyright © 2001 by Jeanne Willis. Illustrations copyright © 2001 by Mark Birchall.

Originally published in 2001 by Andersen Press, Ltd., London, England.

Carolrhoda Books, Inc., a division of Lerner Publishing Group
241 First Avenue North, Minneapolis, MN 55401 U.S.A.

Website address: www.lernerbooks.com

Library of Congress Cataloging-in-Publication Data

Willis, Jeanne.
    No Biting, Puma! / by Jeanne Willis ; illustrated by Mark Birchall.—American ed.
       p. cm.
    Summary: On Puma's first day of school, he keeps biting his classmates until Guinea Pig and Monkey
    teach him a lesson.
    ISBN 1-57505-509-0 (lib. bdg. : alk. paper)
[1. Animals—Fiction. 2. Behavior—Fiction. 3. Schools—Fiction.] I. Birchall, Mark, 1955- ill. II. Title.
PZ7.W68313 No 2001
[E]—dc21   00-012344

Printed and bound in Singapore
1 2 3 4 5 6 - OS - 06 05 04 03 02 01

No Biting, Puma!

By Jeanne Willis
Pictures by Mark Birchall

Carolrhoda Books, Inc./Minneapolis

It was Puma's first day of school.
"School's fun," said the teacher. "You'll
get a taste for it soon."

The minute the teacher turned her back, Puma sneaked up on Elephant and bit his tail.

"Ow!" shrieked Elephant.

And he fell head-first into the box of dress-up clothes.

"Teacher!" shouted Weasel, "Tea . . . cher!
Puma bit Elephant!"
"It wasn't me," said Puma.
"I won't allow biting in this classroom,"
said the teacher.
So Puma did it on the playground instead.

Rabbit had her head down a hole at the time. Her tail was sticking out. Puma just couldn't resist sneaking up and giving it a nip.

"Ouch!" squeaked Rabbit.

"It wasn't me!" said Puma.

Monkey was hanging upside down on the jungle gym. His tail dangled in the long grass.

"Watch out!" squealed Weasel.

But it was too late. Puma sank his teeth into Monkey's tail.

"Ow!" wailed Monkey. "Who did that?"
"It wasn't me," said Puma.

Guinea Pig went to comfort Monkey. "I'm glad that I haven't got a tail," shuddered Guinea Pig. "If I had a tail, Puma would bite me, too."

Monkey thought about this very carefully.
"Turn around a minute," he said.
Monkey looked at the place where Guinea
Pig had no tail and thought of a plan.
"I think I know how to stop Puma from
biting us," he said.
"Can I help?" asked Guinea Pig.
"Enormously," said Monkey. "All we need
is you and a piece of rope."
So they went to look for some.

After recess, it was time to frost cookies.

Puma liked cookies, but not as much as he liked tails! He'd just spotted one he hadn't seen before. It looked a bit ropey, but every time Guinea Pig shifted on his chair, the tail was so twitchy and twisty and tempting that Puma simply had to...

. . . POUNCE!

"Teacher! Tea...cher!" shouted Weasel,
"Someone's bitten Guinea Pig's tail
and it's come right off!"
"Ig woggenk bee!" said Puma.
But it *was* him, because he had a mouth
full of nasty, tough, prickly rope!

Puma looked ashamed.

"It's only a pretend tail," Guinea Pig told him. "You didn't hurt me. But you did hurt Elephant and Rabbit and Monkey."

Puma said, "I'm sorry."

He had only been playing. He hadn't realized how sharp his teeth were.

Then, to show that there were no
hard feelings, Monkey offered Puma
one of his cookies.
"Want a bite?" he said.
But Puma didn't feel like biting
anything just then.